Bleak House

Adapted by
Mary Sebag-Montefiore

Illustrated by Barry Ablett

Reading consultant: Alison Kelly
Roehampton University

Contents

Chapter 1	The plots begin	3
Chapter 2	Esther's diary I	9
Chapter 3	The handwriting	14
Chapter 4	Esther's diary II	23
Chapter 5	A mystery solved	27
Chapter 6	Esther's diary III	36
Chapter 7	Murder	38
Chapter 8	Esther's diary IV	42
Chapter 9	The case is closed	50
Chapter 10	Esther's diary, five years later	61

Chapter 1

The plots begin

Fog. It choked your throat; it hid the shops; it veiled the river. It swirled all over London. It seemed that the sun was dead, and all that was left was the fog and dirt of cold, cruel November.

In the very heart of the fog was Lincoln's Inn Hall. Deep inside the Hall sat the Lord High Chancellor in his wig and gown. All around him lawyers droned on, in the case of *Jarndyce and Jarndyce*. It was about a Will.

Long ago, Mr. Jarndyce had died and left a fortune, but no immediate heir. His cousins had fought for the money in court. Their children and their children's children had fought for it. Lawyers had argued about it for decades. The case of *Jarndyce* stank of trickery and delay. It was as murky as the misty cloak hanging over London.

Far away, in a grand country house, Mr. Tulkinghorn, a family lawyer, had come to see Sir Leicester and Lady Dedlock about that very case.

"If you sign this paper, Lady Dedlock," he said, "it will help your claim."

"But it's so dull," drawled Lady Dedlock, looking bored. "Will *Jarndyce* never end?"

Sir Leicester smiled indulgently. After all their years of marriage she was still beautiful and he adored her.

Lady Dedlock took the piece of paper and her face turned deathly white. "Who... who wrote this?" she stammered, and she slumped to the ground.

"My dear, what's the matter?" Sir Leicester was at her side in an instant.

"I'm fine," she muttered, as she came to. "I just felt faint for a moment."

Mr. Tulkinghorn narrowed his eyes, thinking quickly. Had Lady Dedlock recognized the handwriting? Is that why she 'felt faint'? Perhaps there was an opportunity here for blackmail. He bowed to Sir Leicester and left the room.

As he crossed the hall, he heard a woman snarling like a tigress, "How I hate Lady Dedlock! Now she humiliates me!"

"Who are you?" he asked.

"*Je suis* Hortense," hissed the woman. "Her French maid. She is going to replace me with a village girl. How dare she!"

"I'm sure no one could replace you, Hortense," said Mr. Tulkinghorn. If he could get her on his side, she might help him. "Here is my address," he went on. "I will pay you for any information about Lady Dedlock." His lips stretched in a sinister smile. "After all, it is my duty as the family lawyer to protect Sir Leicester."

"Of course," said Hortense, grinning. She guessed he was lying, but she liked the thought of easy money. "I will be your spy."

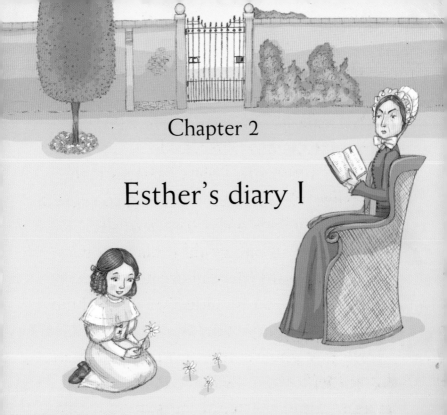

Chapter 2

Esther's diary I

My name is Esther Summerson. All my life I've felt like an outsider. I've never met my parents, I don't even know their names. I was brought up by my godmother, Miss Barbary. Once when I begged her to tell me where I came from, she replied, "Your mother, Esther, is your disgrace, as you are hers. You are set apart. You have no family."

When I was still quite a young woman, Miss Barbary fell ill suddenly and died. I was left with no one and nothing. Then, the day after her burial, her lawyer Mr. Guppy arrived with surprising news.

"My client, Mr. Jarndyce, knew Miss Barbary," he told me. "He promised to be your guardian should anything happen to her. He is inviting you to live with him at Bleak House."

"How wonderful," I gasped in relief. I'd been so worried. At least I wasn't homeless.

Mr. Guppy always stares at me. I think he likes me, but he makes me feel uncomfortable.

Bleak House is huge and grand, beaming with light. And Mr. Jarndyce is so kind, like the father I'd never had. When I arrived, he opened his arms wide and said, "Welcome. You are home." Home! It's such a lovely word.

Two other young people live at Bleak House: Richard and Ada. They are cousins, claimants in the Jarndyce case, like Mr. Jarndyce himself, and both of them orphans like me. Mr. Jarndyce looks after us all.

"Let's be sisters," Ada said to me gleefully. It made me so happy... as if I belonged. Richard is handsome and fun, though restless. First he wanted to be a sailor; now he's training to be a soldier. He joked, "If I win the Jarndyce case, I'll be so rich I'll never do a stroke of work." Silly Richard! Surely it's enough to have a home and be content.

When we were walking in the woods, Mr. Jarndyce said, "Little Woman," — that's become his nickname for me — "if there's anything you want, please tell me." I confided my greatest wish, that I longed to know my background.

In my dreams I find my mother... and she strokes my hair and loves me.

"I only know this," said Mr. Jarndyce. "Your godmother asked me to be your guardian after her death. She said such cruel words about the shame of your existence that I felt sorry for you. I want you to be happy."

As he spoke, a beautiful lady strolled into view. Mr. Jarndyce introduced us. "Lady Dedlock, who lives on the estate next door. Miss Esther Summerson."

Her proud eyes held mine for just one moment, and in that short space of time, though I had never seen her before, I knew her face well. She looked like Miss Barbary, though not so cross. She looked — it was so strange — like me.

*"In Chancery.
Between
John Jarndyce..."*

Chapter 3

The handwriting

Mr. Tulkinghorn went all over
Lincoln's Inn, in and out of the
offices where men sat writing legal
documents. He held the paper that
had caused Lady Dedlock's collapse
before each of them.

"Do you know this handwriting?"
he asked in every office.

At last he found the answer.

"That's Nemo's," said a clerk.
"He lives opposite here, above
Krook's Rag-and-Bottle shop."

"Nemo?" muttered Mr. Tulkinghorn. "But that's Latin for no one..."

The Rag-and-Bottle shop window was crammed with shabby painted signs. Mr. Tulkinghorn pushed open the door, which creaked. Inside were stinking piles of dirty bottles that once held beer, wine, medicine and ink. Beyond them sat an old man and a cat by a dismal fire.

"Are you Krook?" Mr. Tulkinghorn inquired. "I'm looking for Nemo."

"He's upstairs, miserable as usual I expect," Krook grunted. "Take a candle."

Mr. Tulkinghorn climbed into a filthy, empty room. A man with matted hair and bare feet lay on the floor. His skin had a yellow look and a bitter smell hung in the air.

When Mr. Tulkinghorn shook him, there was no response – no breath in the nostrils, no warmth in the body. The man was dead.

Mr. Tulkinghorn searched the room and found a packet of letters tied with a ribbon. He snatched them up and hid them in his coat pocket. Then he went back downstairs.

A thin ragged boy, who looked as if he'd never had a bath in his life, had crept into the shop.

"He's dead," Tulkinghorn said abruptly to Krook. "A drug overdose, I suppose. Who was he?"

Krook shrugged. "I think he was a soldier once. But he lost all his money."

"Did anyone know him?"

"I did," said the boy.

"And you are?" asked Mr. Tulkinghorn.

"Jo," Krook said. "Ain't got no other name. Can't even read. He's a beggar."

Jo turned to Mr. Tulkinghorn. "It's not true! I earn my bread! I sweep horse muck off the streets. Nemo gave me money when he could. He was good to me."

"Ugh!" shuddered Mr. Tulkinghorn, heading for the door. "Just keep away from me, you filthy child."

Mr. Tulkinghorn hurried home to
inspect his find. They were passionate love
letters, all written to a Captain Hawdon
and signed: Honoria Barbary. The letters
told the story of a love affair, of a baby
born to Honoria, young, unmarried, and
now dreading disgrace in the eyes of
society. The baby died. The affair finished.

As the Dedlock family lawyer, Mr.
Tulkinghorn knew that Honoria Barbary
had married and was now... Lady Dedlock.

The very next day, he went to see the Dedlocks in their London house and asked to see Lady Dedlock alone.

"Why alone?" demanded Sir Leicester.

"I don't mind," said Lady Dedlock. "I'm sure it's nothing important."

As soon as Sir Leicester had left the room, Mr. Tulkinghorn turned on Lady Dedlock. "I know who wrote that document," he sneered.

"I'm not interested," said Lady Dedlock, haughtily, freezing her face into an arrogant mask.

"He's dead," Mr. Tulkinghorn went on. "But his name was Captain Hawdon, also known as Nemo. He lived over a shop in Lincoln's Inn and had no friends, except a beggar boy named Jo... And you."

"I have nothing to say."

"Really? I know all your secrets, Lady Dedlock. Your love affair. Your dead baby, born out of marriage. Your disgrace."

Mr. Tulkinghorn's voice was icy with dislike. "Sir Leicester is a proud man. He would never forgive you if your shame became public knowledge."

Lady Dedlock knew this was true. She trembled, though she tried to hide it.

Nothing escaped the lawyer's eyes. It thrilled him to see this haughty woman devastated by his words.

He bowed. "Good-bye, Lady Dedlock. Live with your guilt. One day I shall tell the world that the proud Lady Dedlock is a liar and a fraud."

That evening Sir Leicester asked her, "What did Tulkinghorn want to say to you so privately?"

For one desperate second, she hesitated. She wanted to tell him, but she could not. Fear struggled with honesty, and fear won.

"Nothing important," she said.

Chapter 4

Esther's diary II

I've met the doctor here. His name is Allan Woodcourt. We get along so well. We make each other laugh. He's young and handsome, not in the least like that lawyer, the smarmy Mr. Guppy. And he's thoughtful. He knows Lady Dedlock. He says her pride hides a tortured soul.

We all went, Mr. Jarndyce, Richard, Ada and I, to have tea with Allan's mother. She saw him look at me, and afterwards she took me aside: "I want Allan to marry someone of good family," she said. "We Woodcourts are very proud, you know." She meant, "Keep away from my son." She knows I'm an orphan — just a nobody. I wish I knew where I came from. Mr. Jarndyce noticed my unhappiness, and was extra kind to me.

Richard and Ada are falling in love. Richard is training to be a lawyer now, because he wants to win the Jarndyce case.

"Another career change!" Ada exclaimed. "Why bother with winning Jarndyce? I don't mind being poor."

Richard laughed at her. "I want to be rich!"

"All right," Ada sighed, her eyes huge with love. She can't see that Richard is neither intelligent nor steady. Mr. Jarndyce understands. He thinks it's the uncertainty of the Jarndyce case that has made Richard so indecisive and willing to take risks.

Mr. Guppy comes almost every day. He always says, "Oh Miss Summerson, you do look beautiful!" I'm polite, but I avoid him whenever possible. He's too grovelling.

I don't know why it is, I always seem to be writing about myself. I do mean to write about other people. I hope anyone who reads my diary understands I really don't want to concentrate on myself.

Chapter 5

A mystery solved

Mr. Guppy was so in love with Esther that he wanted to propose. "And I know how to win her heart," he thought. "I'll find her parents. It should be easy enough for a lawyer. Then she'll be so grateful, she'll have to marry me."

The startling discovery he made took him straight to Lady Dedlock in her London house.

"Do you know a Miss Esther Summerson?" he asked.

"I have met her," said Lady Dedlock.

"The person who brought her up was named Miss Barbary. She said she was Esther's godmother. In fact, she was her aunt — and your sister. Esther Summerson's real name is Esther Hawdon. Her father was a law writer, who died a short while ago at Krook's in Lincoln's Inn. And her mother is... you."

For a moment, Lady Dedlock was stunned into silence.

"Please go," she begged him. When she was alone, she went to her bedroom and wept, thankful that Sir Leicester, in his study, could not hear her tears through the thick walls.

"My child, my child," she sobbed in agony. "Not dead in the first hours of life as my cruel sister told me, but alive. Brought up by my sister, who told me she'd never see me again after my disgrace. Oh Esther, my child."

Lady Dedlock now desperately wished for two things: one, to see her dead love's grave, and two, to embrace her daughter.

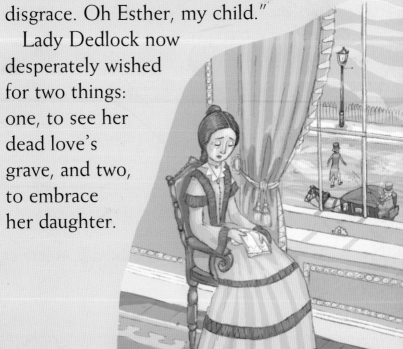

Quickly she disguised herself, slipping on a shabby black dress belonging to Hortense, her maid. No one would recognize her, or even see her. It was almost dark; the short winter afternoon was extinguished by clouds of sooty chimney smoke and fog.

She made her way to Lincoln's Inn and Krook's shop. Outside the entrance, a ragged boy swept the frosty street.

"Are you Jo?" she asked him, remembering Mr. Tulkinghorn's words.

"Yep, my lady."

"I'm not a lady. I'm a servant."

"Huh!" said Jo, because he could see her hands were white and soft, not rough with work.

"Tell me, Jo, do you know where Nemo is buried?"

Jo nodded.

"If you show me, I'll give you more money than you've ever had in your life."

Shouldering his broom, Jo led her through an ugly archway to a rusty iron gate, where rats scuttled in the misty swirls of fog. Beyond the gate was a graveyard. The gate was locked.

"They put him there," said Jo. "The paupers' ground."

She strained her eyes in the darkness, shuddering at the stench. "Is it blessed?" she asked.

Jo stared. "Dunno. Don't make the bones any different if it's blessed or not."

Lady Dedlock wept again, mourning the tragedy of Captain Hawdon's wasted life, and remembering how they had loved each other so many years ago. Then she pulled herself together, gave Jo some money, and walked away. Finding herself outside Mr. Tulkinghorn's house, on an impulse, she rang the bell.

Mr. Tulkinghorn himself answered the door. "What do you want, Lady Dedlock?" he asked. He could not read her eyes. Was it fear or anger that made them flash?

"I've decided to run away," she told him. "My husband will be horrified when he discovers that I, whom he so admires, have brought shame to his name. My disappearance will only be a relief to him. I have left my jewels behind. And you see I wear my servant's dress, so no one will know me."

"If you disappear," Mr. Tulkinghorn replied, "you will make it a hundred times more obvious that you have a wicked secret. I may reveal it. I may not. But you'd be wise to stay put."

"I will do as I think best," she flung at him, storming out. But as soon as she shut the front door, her brave, challenging manner vanished. Her face was twisted in distress, she clasped her hands behind her head, her hair flew wild and undone.

She sped to Mr. Jarndyce's London house, praying that Esther was there.

"Lady Dedlock!" Esther exclaimed, amazed, as she opened the door.

"Come, my child," urged Lady Dedlock. "Never mind the cold and fog; let's go to the garden. I have something secret – but so important – to tell you."

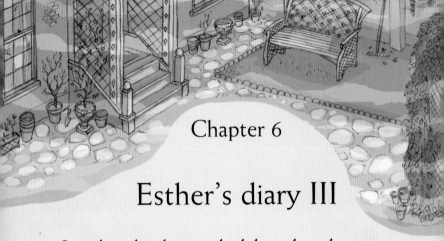

Chapter 6

Esther's diary III

Something has happened while we have been staying with Mr. Jarndyce in his London house. Something amazing... and shattering. Lady Dedlock came. "I have something to tell you," she said. We went to the garden. She took me in her arms, kissed me, and then she cried, "Oh my child, forgive me! I am your unhappy, wicked mother!"

I begged her to stop crying. I told her I'd always longed to know my mother. Whatever she'd done, she had my forgiveness — my heart overflowed with love.

"It's too late," she murmured. "I must travel my dark road alone. I am beyond help. I have brought disgrace to those I love."

"No!" I insisted.

"I was told you died at birth," she continued. "My sister took you from me, and brought you up, hidden from me. If I had only known! But, darling child, these kisses must be for the last time. We shall never meet again. I cannot let my husband suffer for my wrongs. People are so cruel. They would mock him and I can't let that happen. It's better if I disappear."

I could not persuade her otherwise. As quickly as she came, she left. I was shaken. Would it have been better if I had never been born? If I had not breathed, would the world have been happier?

I wish I were at Bleak House, not here in London. Whenever I am unhappy or hurt, I always feel at peace there, sheltered in its walls. It is truly home.

Chapter 7

Murder

After Lady Dedlock's visit, Mr. Tulkinghorn remained in his study. He wondered about going for a walk, but decided it was too foggy.

Thoughtfully, he drew the curtains. If only the window had reflected not the fog but the future and warned him: "Leave the house!" If only the curtains had whispered one word to him: "Go!"

Again the doorbell rang. This time it was Lady Dedlock's maid. She slipped inside, as excited as a wild cat. "I, Hortense, take my revenge on Lady Dedlock," she hissed. "You promised you would reward me for information about her. So I will tell you: she has run away, wearing my clothes. Now pay me."

"But I already know that," said Mr. Tulkinghorn. "I owe you nothing."

"Give me money," she shrieked.

Mr. Tulkinghorn decided that Hortense was no longer useful to him. "If you ever come here again demanding money, I will send for the police," he snapped.

"If you do that," cried Hortense, shaking her fist, "I will prove to them that you are a wicked cheat!"

"Be careful with your threats," Mr. Tulkinghorn began menacingly, and a gun shot rang out.

He slumped in his chair, a red stain spreading from his heart. Hortense flew from the room, swift and silent, like an animal on the run.

Chapter 8

Esther's diary IV

Mr. Guppy has proposed! He sank down on one knee. I said "No," because I don't love him at all. Everything here is sad and mixed-up right now. You know how Mr. Jarndyce has been so good to Richard, paying for his training and giving him a home. Now Richard says he will fight Mr. Jarndyce in court to win the Jarndyce case. Mr. Jarndyce is very upset.

"How could you?" Ada sobbed to Richard.

"I've got big debts," Richard confided.

"Debts?" repeated Ada. "Why? I don't understand."

Richard smiled. He has such a sunny manner. "I like living well. What's wrong with having everything I want? I need to win the case to pay my bills. Don't bother your pretty little head about business, Ada."

Oh, Richard! I so wish you weren't like that.

I told Mr. Jarndyce that Mr. Guppy had discovered my parents, but I kept my mother's secret and did not say who she was.

"I'm glad you've learned the truth at last," Mr. Jarndyce said. "Be proud of who you are, Little Woman." He is so wise.

Allan Woodcourt came to visit. While we were talking, the doorbell rang. It was Mr. Bucket, the police inspector. "The lawyer Mr. Tulkinghorn has been murdered," he announced.

"On the night in question, Jo the road sweeper says a lady dressed like a servant spoke to him, before going in to see Mr. Tulkinghorn. And then she visited you. That lady is Lady Dedlock, who has since disappeared. It is a most interesting coincidence."

I saw he suspected my mother of murder! It could
not be true. "Lady Dedlock was unhappy, not
angry," I said. "Let me talk to this Jo," I added.
"Maybe he'll tell me more than he told you."

"I'll come too," Allan said.

We went together through the streets to Lincoln's
Inn and found Jo, lying on the pavement and
shivering with fever.

"Why aren't you at home, in bed?" I asked.

"Ain't got no home!" he muttered, coughing.

It's dreadful that children like Jo are ragged and starving. Something's wrong with the world when the rich are too rich and the poor are so unhappy. "Come with me, Jo," I said. "I'll take care of you."

I took him back home and nursed him. He had smallpox, Allan said. When he was slightly better, he told me that he had shown my mother Nemo's graveyard — he told me where it was — then said he followed her and saw her enter and leave Mr. Tulkinghorn's house. Later another woman went in, muttering, "I, Hortense, take my revenge on Lady Dedlock," and he heard a pistol shot.

I told Mr. Bucket, and he is going to arrest Hortense, my mother's maid, for murder.

Catastrophe has hit us. Jo was getting worse, growing more fragile with every hour.

"It's very dark," he said last night, as I sat with him by candlelight. His eyes were now too weak to see; I could tell his life was fading fast. Stroking his hand, I said, "Our Father, which art in Heaven."

"Our Father," whispered Jo, as softly as a leaf falling from a tree... then he was silent. Poor boy, killed by disease, poverty and neglect. I can't bear it. I can't stop shivering. It must be because I'm so unhappy. My head aches.

***

I haven't written my diary for weeks, because I've been ill. I caught smallpox from Jo. This morning, I asked Ada for a mirror so I could brush my hair.

"No, Esther," she said. "No mirror for you."

"Why?" I asked. She turned away, weeping. But I made her bring one. I had to see what was so terrible about me that I couldn't look in a mirror. As soon as I glanced in the glass, I understood.

Smallpox has scarred my face — I think forever. I am ugly... so ugly... Mr. Jarndyce says there's no difference really, because I'm still the same person underneath it all. Wise though he is, I can't believe him. I'm miserable. Allan will never think me pretty now.

Ada told me that she and Richard secretly married while I was ill. "He's made lots of wrong decisions," she said, "but because I love him, I'll support him, rich or poor. He's still hoping to win the Jarndyce case."

I couldn't help a twinge of envy. Ada has Richard. I'm so hideous, no one will ever want me.

Chapter 9

The case is closed

Sir Leicester Dedlock sat alone in his house in the country, unable to sleep or eat properly. "If only my wife would come back," he repeated again and again. "Whatever she's done, I love her. I wish she'd come home."

No one could comfort him. No one knew where she was. He thought of her all the time, picturing her cold, hungry and lonely, until he turned from his imaginings with a howl of misery to cry once more, "I would forgive you – everything. Come back, come back."

Esther remained in London, too ill to
return to Bleak House. Gradually, she
recovered and her scars began to fade.
Allan Woodcourt came to visit her often...

"I don't want his pity," Esther thought.
"I wish he wouldn't come. I'm not pretty
enough for him. Why can't he stay away?"

"Have you heard the news?" Allan asked on his next visit.

"Tell us," replied Mr. Jarndyce, glad of any diversion to cheer Esther up.

"*Jarndyce and Jarndyce* is over. The case is finished."

"But who has won?" asked Mr. Jarndyce.

"No one," Allan explained. "The money finally ran out. It all disappeared into the lawyers' pockets, because the case had lasted for so many years. There's not a penny left!"

"Poor Richard!" exclaimed Esther.

"Best thing that could have happened to him," comforted Mr. Jarndyce. "Now he knows *Jarndyce* is over, he'll be much steadier. Ada will be happier, too."

"What about you, Mr. Jarndyce?" asked Esther. "It means you'll never be rich either."

"I don't mind," he smiled. "I have enough for my needs. Who needs more?"

"Will you come for a walk, Esther?" Allan asked.

"Oh, no..." she replied, quickly, touching her face.

"Go, my dear," urged Mr. Jarndyce. "Your scars are barely noticeable. You're looking so much better."

"We can go where you like," Allan encouraged her.

Esther considered. "I'd like to see my father's grave. Jo told me where he's buried," she said.

"We'll go now," Allan promised.

On the way, he asked her to marry him.

"B... but Allan," she stuttered, torn between surprise and delight, "I look so horrible. I thought you could never..."

"The scars don't matter. I've always loved you, anyway."

"But... I am..." The terrible words she had heard in her childhood still haunted her. "I am my mother's disgrace."

"I know the secret," Allan assured her. "Mr. Guppy told Mr. Jarndyce, who told me. I met your mother, and admired her. I love you, Esther, because your heart is soft and your mind is strong, and you are kind to rich and poor alike. So, will you...?"

"Oh yes! I love you too. I always have."

They had reached the entrance to the graveyard, but a crowd had collected there, blocking the way.

The crowd surrounded a woman who was lying by the gate, one arm hooked through it, as though she embraced it.

"Let me through," cried Allan. "I'm a doctor."

He knelt by the woman's side, and Esther saw a look of compassion on his face. "Come, darling," he said to Esther. "Yours should be the first hands to touch her."

Resolutely Esther crept forward, though she was full of foreboding. She lifted the head, and turned the face. It was her mother, cold and dead. By her side was a note.

This place where I lie down has often been in my mind. Farewell. Forgive.

Chapter 10

Esther's diary, five years later

To anyone who reads my diary, I want it to be known — after sadness and tragedy there is happiness. Joy is stronger than despair.

Allan and I love each other so much. He is a wonderful husband. Mr. Jarndyce has been extraordinarily kind, too. When I told him that Allan had proposed, he said, "Little Woman, if I were younger, I would have married you myself. Allan Woodcourt is a fortunate man. I want to give you a wedding present. I know you love Bleak House. It is yours. I pray you will be blessed with children and that the sun will shine upon your marriage forever."

And all this came true...

"Esther," said Allan this morning, drawing my arm through his. "Do you look in the glass?"

"You know I do," I frowned. "You see me do it."

"Don't you know you are prettier than you ever were?"

"I'm not sure that's true," I laughed. "But I do know that I have two pretty daughters and a handsome husband, and that's quite enough beauty for one house."

Charles Dickens 1812-1870

Charles Dickens lived in London, England, during the reign of Queen Victoria. When he was twelve, he was sent to work in a factory. He never forgot how hard life could be and his novels highlighted the huge gap between the rich and poor.

Dickens went on to become one of the most famous writers of his time. His other tales include *Oliver Twist*, *Great Expectations*, *A Christmas Carol*, *A Tale of Two Cities* and *David Copperfield*.

Usborne Quicklinks

To find out more about Dickens and life in Victorian times, go to the Usborne Quicklinks Website at www.usborne-quicklinks.com Read the internet safety guidelines, and then type the keywords "Bleak House".

Edited by Katie Daynes
Designed by Michelle Lawrence
Series editor: Lesley Sims
Series designer: Russell Punter